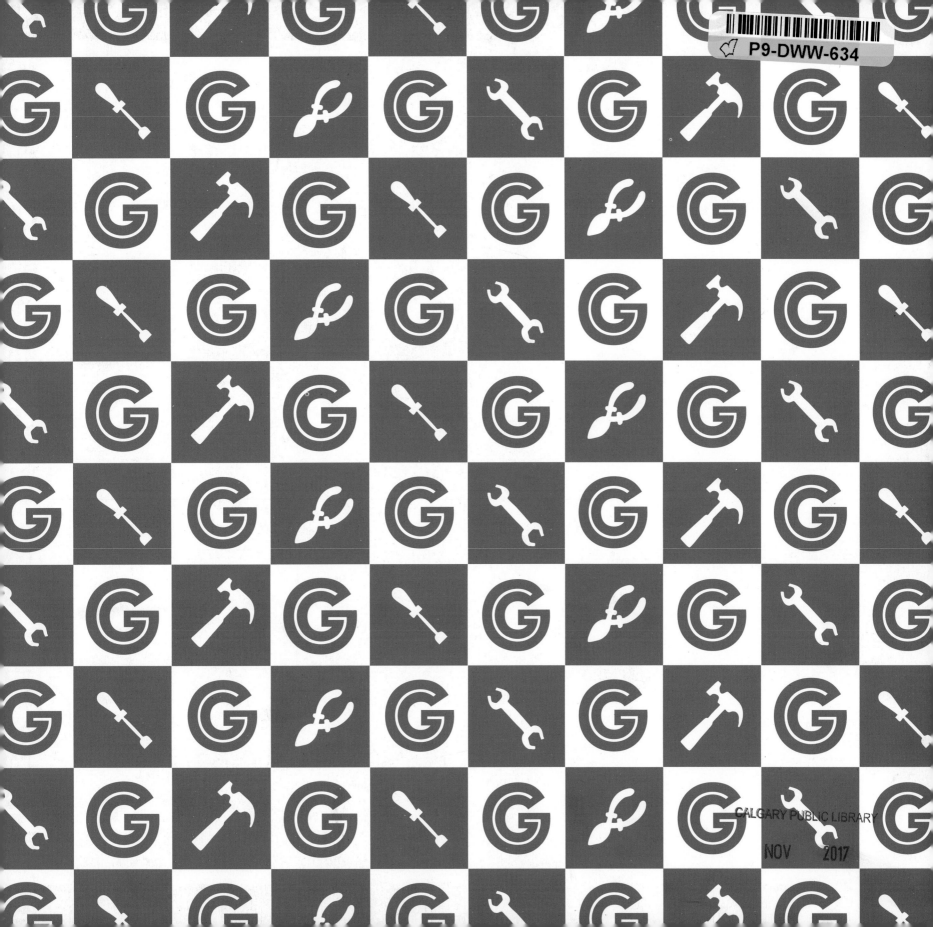

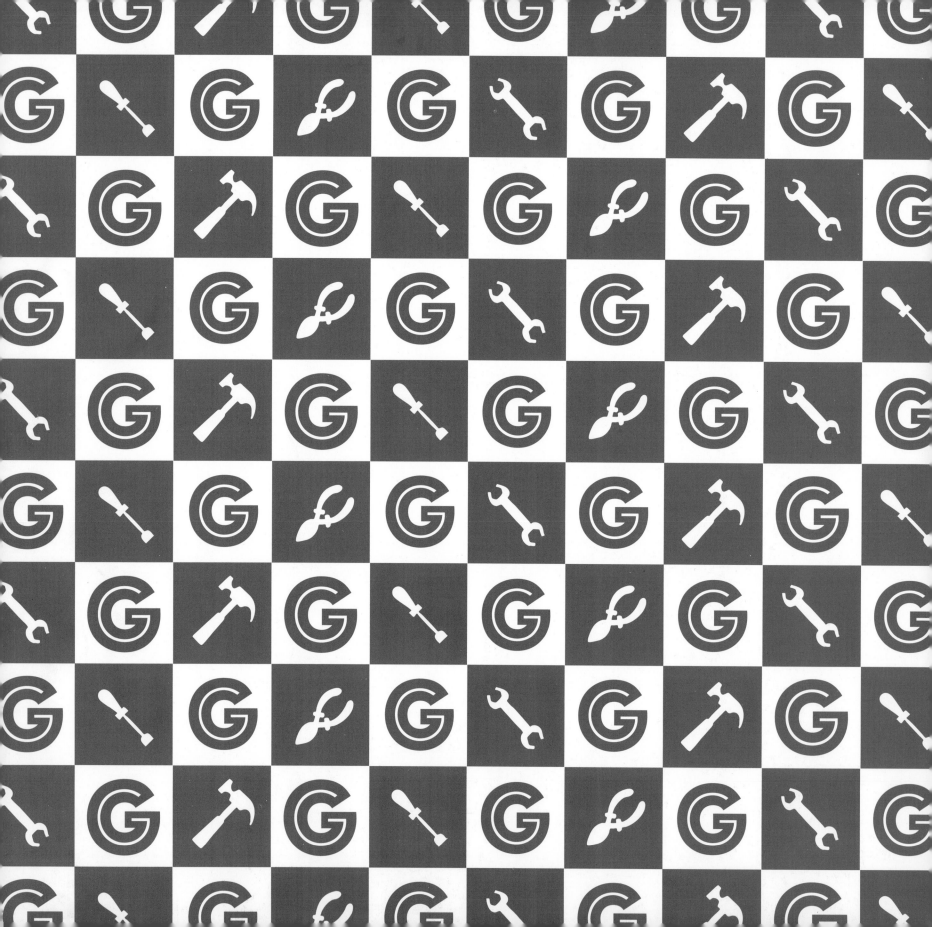

This book belongs to

....

....

GUS'S GARAGE

Leo Timmers

GECKO PRESS

Here comes Gus. The things he stores!

Whatever will he use them for?

"Hey there, Rico. How's it going?"

"Gus, this seat—I'm overflowing."

"Let's see. I have some bits and bobs.

This goes with that. There. Just the job!"

"Gina, how's the view up there?"

"Chilly, Gus—I need warm air."

"Let's see. I have some bits and bobs.

This goes with that. There. Just the job!"

"Hello, Walter. You look dry."

"Gus, my skin—it's going to fry."

"Let's see. I have some bits and bobs.

This goes with that. There. Just the job!"

"Miss P. A hot pink situation?"

"Gus, I need refrigeration."

"Let's see. I have some bits and bobs.

This goes with that. There. Just the job!"

"Hello, Henry—here at last."

"Gus, I'm going nowhere fast."

"Let's see. I have some bits and bobs.

This goes with that. There. Just the job!"

Day is done. What's left to do?

Gus needs water, soap, shampoo...

He joins the last few bits and bobs.

This goes with that.

There. Just the job!

First American edition published in 2017
by Gecko Press USA, an imprint of Gecko Press Ltd

This edition first published in 2016 by Gecko Press
PO Box 9335, Marion Square, Wellington 6141, New Zealand
info@geckopress.com

Distributed in the United States and Canada
by Lerner Publishing Group
www.lernerbooks.com
Distributed in the United Kingdom
by Bounce Sales and Marketing
www.bouncemarketing.co.uk
Distributed in Australia by Scholastic Australia
www.scholastic.com.au
Distributed in New Zealand by Upstart Distribution
www.upstartpress.co.nz

This book was published with the support of the
Flemish Literature Fund
www.flemishliterature.be

English text by James Brown
Typesetting by Vida & Luke Kelly, New Zealand
Printed in China by Everbest Printing Co. Ltd,
an accredited ISO 14001 & FSC certified printer

ISBN hardback: 978-1-776570-92-8
ISBN paperback: 978-1-776570-93-5
Ebook available

For more curiously good books visit geckopress.com

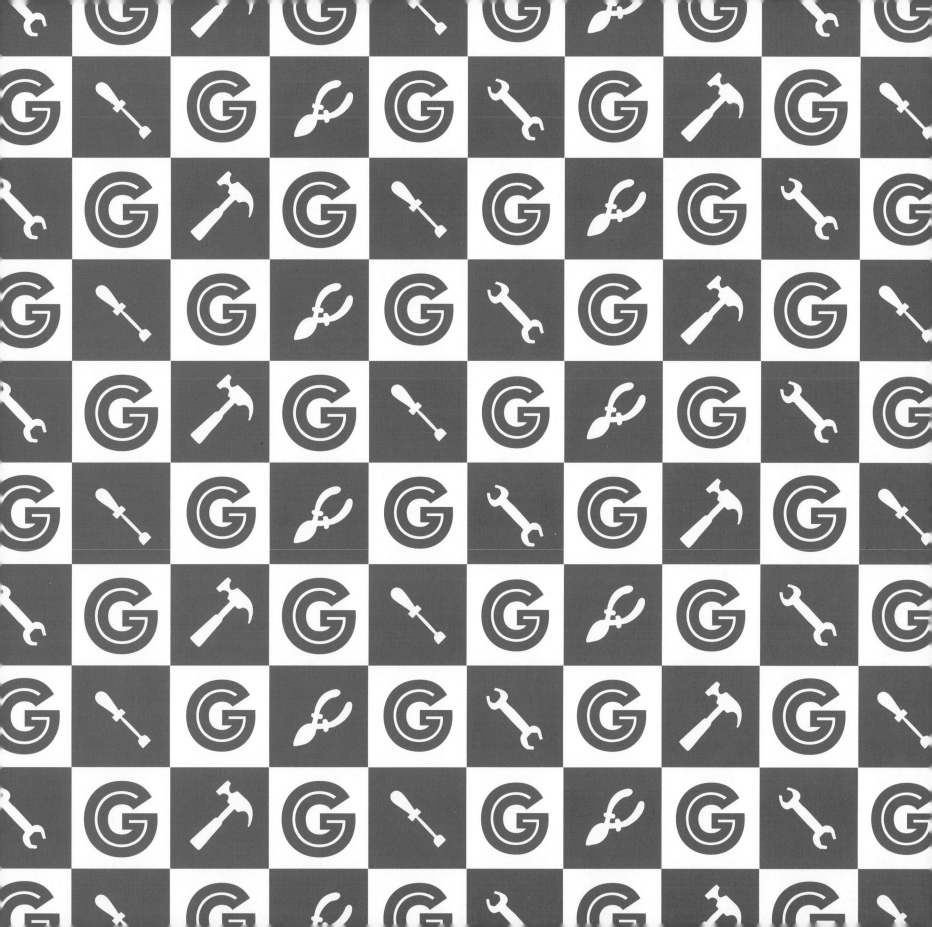

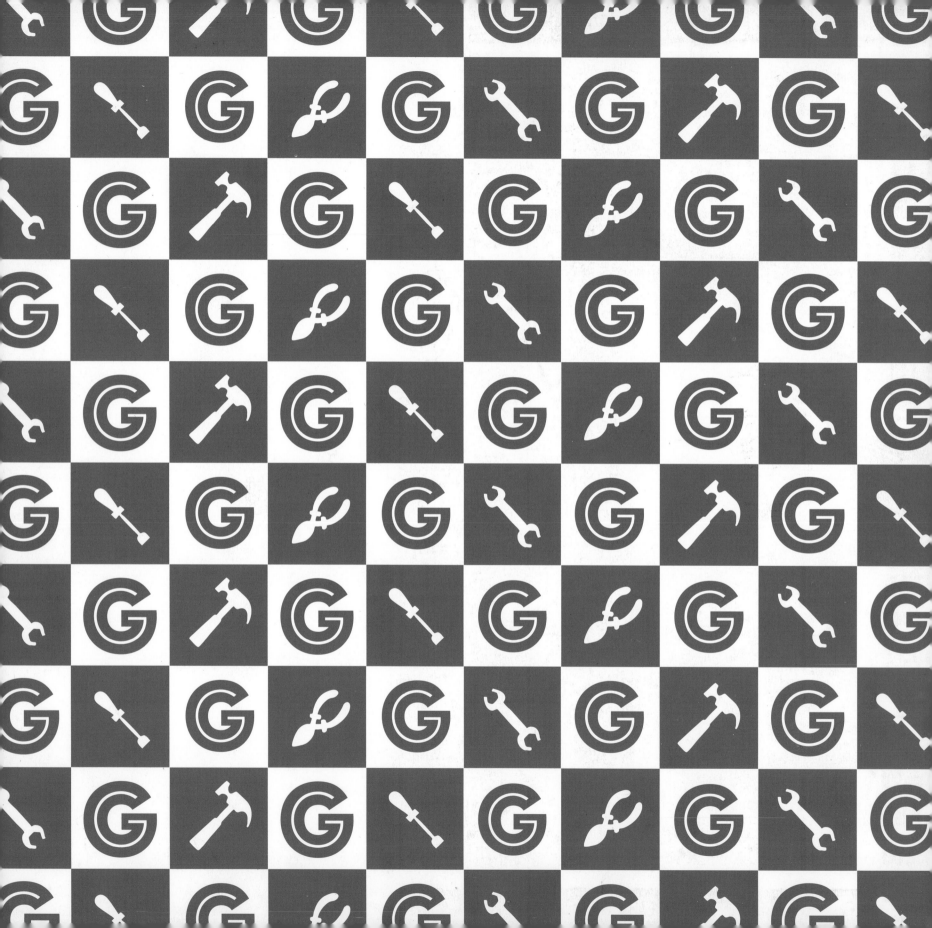